Tales from The Wind in the Willows

For Bertie, Sophia and Louis
S.M.
For Andrew, Richard, Christopher, Helen, Katie and Emily
G.P.

This edition first published in the United Kingdom in 2001
by David Bennett Books Limited, an imprint of Chrysalis Books plc,
64 Brewery Road, London N7 9NT
Originally published as six separate titles in 1995.
Text copyright © 1995 Stella Maidment.
Illustrations copyright © 1995 Graham Philpot.
Style and design copyright © 2001 David Bennett Books Limited.
Stella Maidment asserts her moral right to be
identified as the author of this work.
Graham Philpot asserts his moral right to be
identified as the illustrator of this work.

This edition published by Barnes & Noble, Inc.

2002 Barnes & Noble Books

ISBN 0-7607-3376-7

Printed and bound in Singapore

10 9 8 7 6 5 4 3 2 1

Tales from The Wind in the Willows

Based on the original story by
Kenneth Grahame

Retold by
Stella Maidment

Illustrated by
Graham Philpot

BARNES
&NOBLE
BOOKS
NEW YORK

CONTENTS

The Wind in the Willows

Kenneth Grahame was born in 1859 in Edinburgh. His mother died when he was just four years old. After her death, Kenneth lived with his grandmother in Cookham Dean, a village near the River Thames in Berkshire.

At the age of nine, he was sent to a boarding school in Oxford. Kenneth loved his school days and spent much of his free time discovering the city of Oxford and exploring the River Thames in a canoe. When he left school, Kenneth began

working as a clerk for the Bank of England.

In 1899 he married Elspeth Thomson and the following year the couple had their only child, Alastair. Kenneth began telling his son bedtime stories about moles and water rats; it was from these stories that *The Wind in the Willows* developed.

The Wind in the Willows was published in 1908. At first the book was not a great success, but by the mid-1920s its popularity had grown and it had been reprinted more than 20 times.

 $\mathcal{M}$ole is the character we meet first in *The Wind in the Willows*. He is a shy, home-loving animal and leads a sheltered, quiet life… until he meets Ratty. Together with Ratty, Mole embarks upon a series of adventures – sometimes pleasant and sometimes quite terrifying, but always memorable!

When Toad gets into some of his more difficult scrapes, Mole joins the other riverbank animals in coming to his aid.

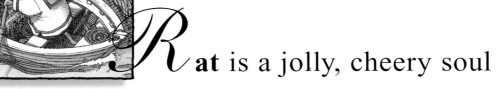

Rat is a jolly, cheery soul who enjoys life on the river. He loves simple pleasures – picnicking in the warm sunshine or sitting in a cosy armchair by the fireplace.

Ratty is pleased to make friends with Mole – he has always wanted a friend with whom he can explore the river… and beyond. He is a loyal companion and can always be relied upon to help a friend in need.

Otter, another one of the riverbank creatures, sees the good in everyone… even Toad! He is quite timid and doesn't join Rat and Mole in their escapades. Instead he is quite happy to stay in the safety of his riverbank home.

We meet Otter for the first time when Rat and Mole are rowing down the river for their picnic. He reappears just once more – at the banquet held in honor of Toad's triumphant return to Toad Hall.

 **The** irrepressible but lovable Toad lives in the splendor of Toad Hall. He hurtles from one craze to the next and sometimes gets himself into terrible trouble. At one stage he even ends up in a prison cell and his beloved home is overrun by enemies.

Toad can always rely on the help of his faithful riverbank friends and, by the end of the story, he is restored to his former glory.

Badger lives on the edge of the Wild Wood. He is a kindly, dependable animal and a friendly face in the midst of strange, threatening territory. He behaves as a father-figure to the other animals and usually takes control in difficult or dangerous situations.

Badger can be quite firm with Toad, in order to curb his wayward tendencies, but this is because he has only Toad's best interests at heart.

**T**he stoats, weasels and ferrets are the shady inhabitants of the Wild Wood. They do not live by the polite, gentlemanly code shared by Rat, Mole, Toad, Otter and Badger.

When they seize Toad Hall, the ferrets guard the front gates ferociously with guns and other weapons while gangs of stoats and weasels run amok inside, breaking furniture and defacing Toad's treasured collection of paintings.

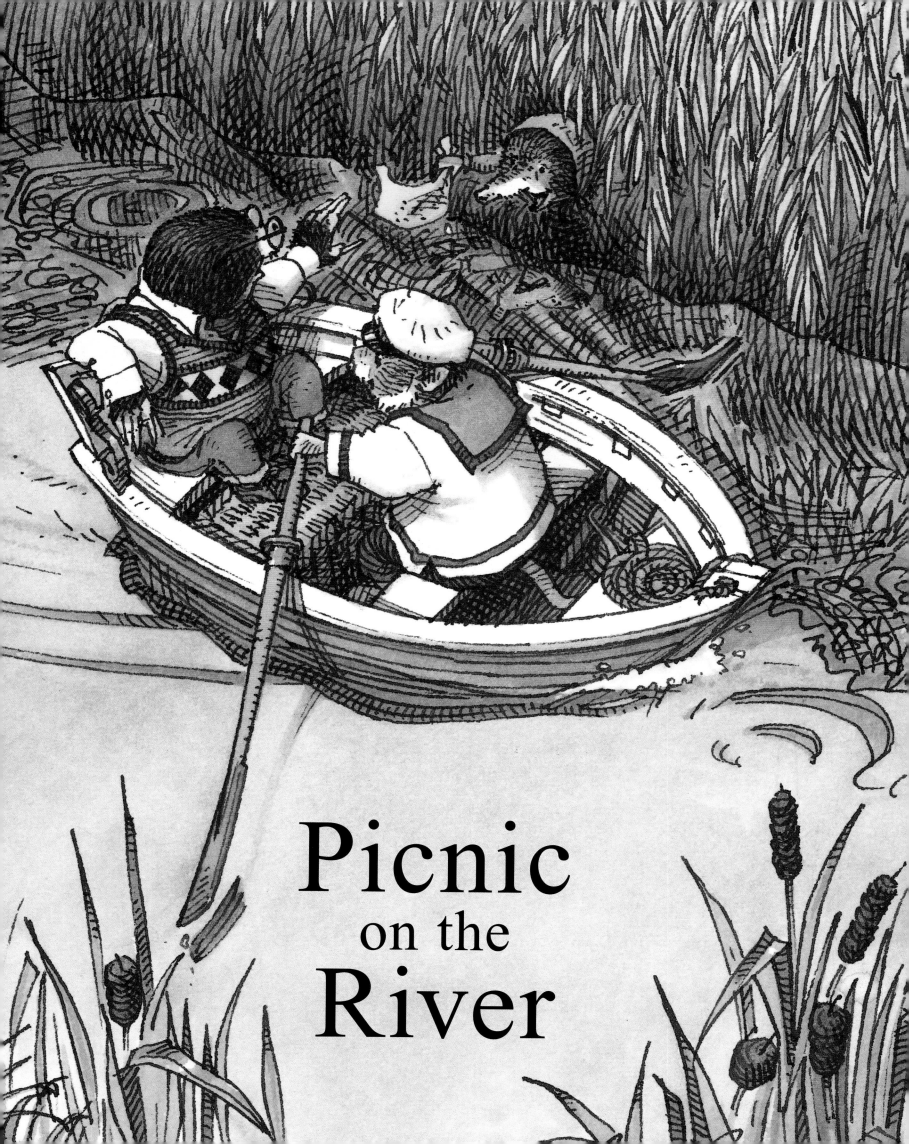

Picnic
on the
River

*M*ole had been working hard all
morning, spring-cleaning and brightening
his little home. He had swept and dusted
and now he was painting the ceiling.
His back ached and his arms were weary.
Suddenly he threw down his brush.

"I've had enough of all this spring-
cleaning!" he said.

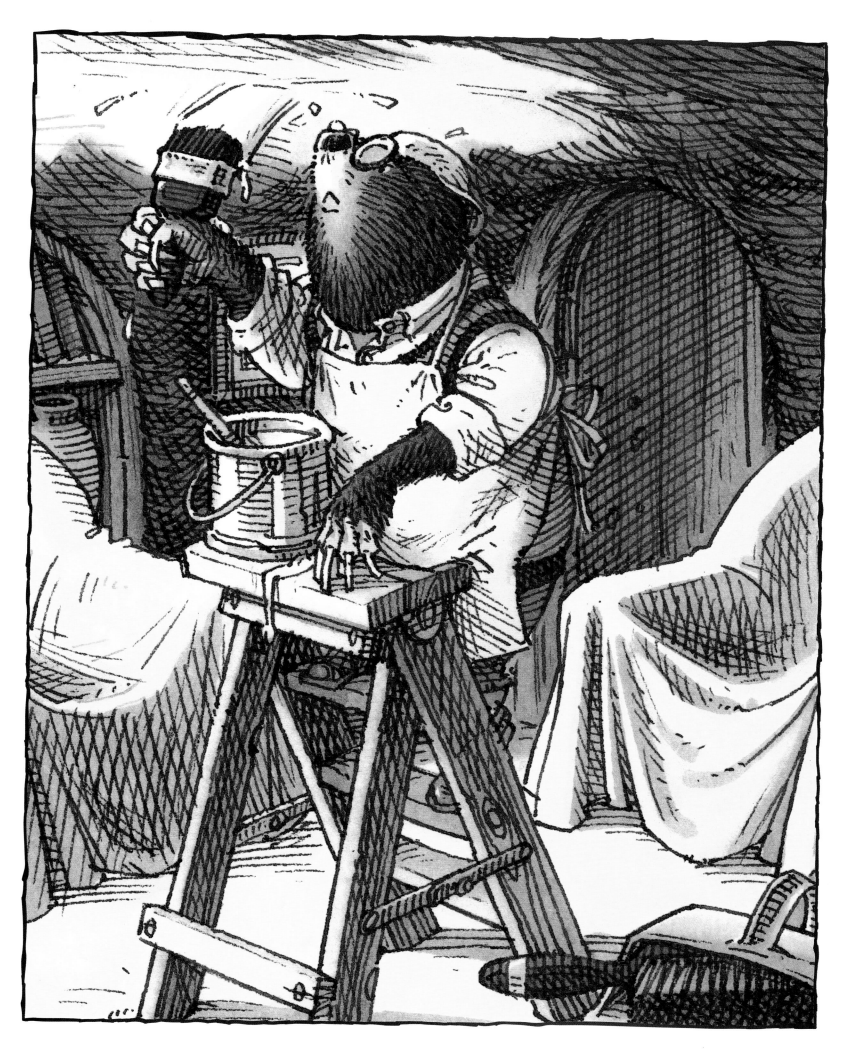

He scrambled up the tunnel that led to his front door and was soon rolling in the grass outside.

"This is great!" he said. "This is better than whitewashing!"

The sun was shining and the birds sang. Mole jumped high in the air and hurried off across the meadow.

Suddenly he came to a deep, rushing
river. He watched it bubbling and swirling
and was bewitched. Then he saw
something move on the opposite bank.
It was the Water Rat!

"Want a lift over?" Rat asked,
nodding towards a little rowing boat.

"This is wonderful!" said Mole,
climbing aboard. "I've never been
in a boat before!"

"Then you haven't lived!" said Rat
in amazement. "Believe me,
my friend, there is nothing
– *absolutely* nothing –
like messing about in boats.
Come with me and
see for yourself!"

The two animals set off down the river, Rat rowing with neat, brisk strokes while Mole sat in a dreamy silence.

"So – this – is – a – river!" he said at last.

"*The* River," corrected Rat, "and my world! I live by it and with it, on it and in it. I wouldn't want anything else!"

Soon it was time for lunch. Rat fastened the boat to the bank and Mole unpacked the picnic basket.

"Pitch in, old fellow!" said Rat.

It seemed a long time since breakfast.

After a while Mole noticed a streak
of bubbles travelling along the water.
Then a glistening muzzle appeared.
It was the Otter.

"All the world seems to be out on the
river today," he said. "Look at Toad over
there in his brand new rowing boat –
new clothes, new everything."

"So that's his latest craze!" laughed
Rat and waved as a short, stout figure
flashed into view, rowing hard but
splashing badly.

"First it was sailing, then punting.

Last year it was house-boats."

"Such a good fellow, too," said Otter.

"But no stability – especially in a boat!"

On the way home Mole asked if he could try rowing.

"Not yet," smiled Rat. "You'll need some lessons first."

But Mole, full of lunch and confidence, jumped up and seized the oars. But, as he tried to row, he lost his balance and – SPLOOSH – they were both in the river!

The cold water sang in Mole's ears as he felt himself sinking, down and down. Then a firm paw gripped the back of his neck. It was Rat – and Mole could *feel* him laughing. Rat propelled the helpless animal to shore and hauled him out, a squashy, miserable, wet lump.

Rat swiftly righted the boat and rescued the picnic basket.

Mole was deeply ashamed.

"I'm very sorry, Ratty," he said.

"That's all right!" laughed Rat. "What's a little wet to a Water Rat? But look here! Why don't you come and stay with me for a while? I could teach you to row and to swim as well."

So back they went to Rat's house. Rat made a fire in the parlor and lent Mole a dressing gown and slippers.

Then, after supper, Mole fell asleep in the best bedroom, listening to his new friend, the River, lapping against the window outside.

The
Open Road

One bright morning Mole found Rat
playing with the ducks by the river.

"I was wondering," began Mole,
"could we go and call on Mr Toad?
I've heard he's a very nice animal."

"Certainly!" said Rat. "Get the boat
out and we'll paddle up there at once."

So they set off in the boat and,
rounding a bend in the river, they soon
came to a handsome old house with
well-kept lawns stretching down to
the water's edge.

"That's Toad Hall," explained Rat.
"Those are the stables and that's the
banqueting hall on the left. Toad is
rather rich, you know."

They found Toad in the garden.

"Hooray!" he cried, leaping up and shaking their paws warmly. "This is splendid! You're the very animals I wanted to see. I've given up boating now, and I've found the only thing I ever want to do for the rest of my life."

"Come and see!"

He led them to the stable yard and pointed proudly to a beautiful yellow gypsy caravan with shiny, green-and-red trimmings.

Inside there were little sleeping bunks, a folding table, a stovetop, bookshelves, all sorts of pots and pans and cupboards filled with food.

"What could be better?" cried Toad. "The whole world before us and a horizon that's always changing! Let's leave this afternoon!"

Toad could be very persuasive. Before Rat and Mole knew it, the old gray horse was harnessed to the caravan and they were ready to go.

By evening they were miles from home.
They ate their dinner sitting on the grass.

Toad talked importantly about all
the things he meant to do, while stars
grew bright in the sky around them
and the yellow moon came up to keep
them company.

But that night, lying in his bunk, Rat
missed the sounds of his riverbank home.

"We'll go back tomorrow, if you like,"
whispered Mole.

"No," said Rat. "This craze of Toad's
won't last. They never do. Soon
something else will take its place.
We'll wait until then. Good night!"

And Rat was right! Two days later they were strolling along the road, Mole in front with the horse, Toad talking non-stop as usual, when suddenly they heard a faint 'poop-poop' in the distance.

Glancing back, they saw a cloud of dust coming towards them at incredible speed.

A moment later there was a blast of wind and a whirl of sound that made them jump for the nearest ditch. It was upon them! A huge glittering motor car roared past, flinging up clouds of dust as it disappeared into the distance. Then it was gone.

The poor, startled horse plunged and reared. With a heart-rending crash the canary-yellow caravan, until that moment Toad's pride and joy, fell sideways into the ditch and lay broken beyond repair.

Rat danced about in a fury.
"You villains!" he shouted.
"I'll have the law onto you!"

Mole tried to
calm the horse.

But Toad sat staring ahead as if
in a trance. With a happy smile
on his face he was
murmuring faintly
to himself,
"Poop-poop!
Poop-poop!"

"Come on," said Rat grimly.

"We shall just have to walk to the nearest town. There's nothing to be done with Toad. He's quite hopeless. He's forgotten all about his caravan. He's found a new craze now!"

But that is another story…

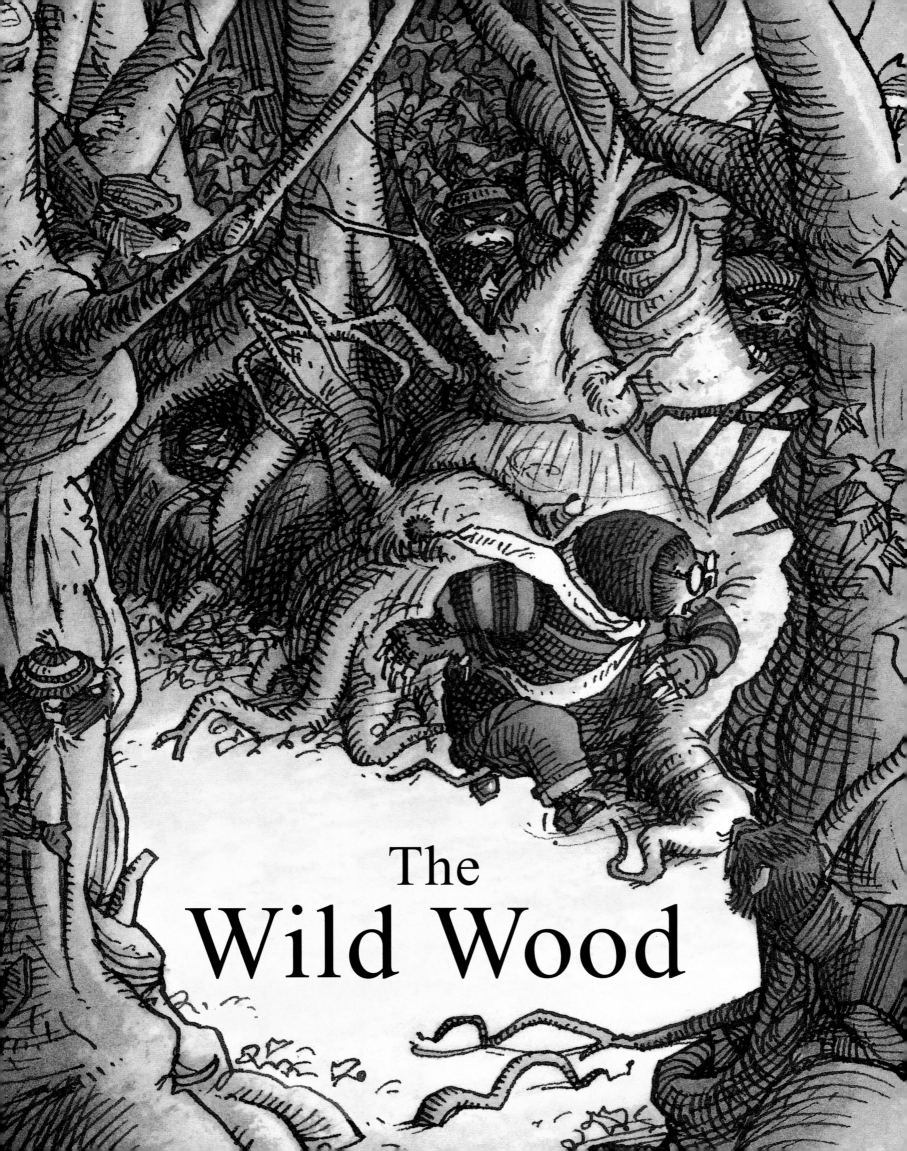

The Wild Wood

"You know, Ratty," said Mole one day,
"I've heard such a lot about Badger.
Couldn't we go and visit him?"

"Oh no!" cried Rat, looking alarmed.
"He lives in the Wild Wood. It's not
a place for visitors. And, besides,
he's very shy. He'll turn up sometime,
he always does."

Mole waited and waited. Summer turned to winter and the days grew cold and dark, but Badger never came along.

One day, as Rat sat dozing by the fire, Mole decided he could wait no longer. He tiptoed out of the parlor into the cold gray afternoon air.

Dusk was falling as Mole walked into the wood.

Twigs crackled under his feet and
logs tripped him. Then the faces began.
Sharp little faces peering out of the bank
– first one, then another – staring with
hard bright eyes. Mole walked faster,
turning off the path.

Then came the pattering. First it
sounded like falling leaves but the
pat-pat-pat of tiny feet grew louder and
faster until Mole felt the whole wood
was running – hunting, chasing, closing in.

In a panic Mole started running too…

At last, when he could run no further,
he fell into the hollow of an old beech tree.

As he lay there, panting and trembling
in the darkness, he understood, too late,
what Rat had tried to keep from him –
the Terror of the Wild Wood!

Meanwhile Rat woke suddenly and looked about for his friend. He found Mole's footprints in the mud outside and saw them leading straight for the Wild Wood.

Then Rat looked very grave. He took two pistols and a club and set off at a quick pace.

Rat searched the woods for more than an hour, calling, "Moly, Moly! Where are you?"

At last he heard an answering cry. He found the hollow tree and crept inside. There was Mole, exhausted and trembling with fear. "Oh Ratty!" cried Mole. "I'm so glad to see you!"

Rat let Mole rest until he was strong
enough to brave the woods again.
Then he climbed up to look outside.

"Hello!" said Rat. "It's snowing hard!"

Mole came and crouched beside him.
Everything had changed. The dark wood
was filled with a gleaming carpet of light.

"We'll have to try to find our
way home," said Mole.

They set out bravely, holding
on to each other and looking for
familiar paths, but it was useless.

Two hours later they were tired,
cold and hopelessly lost.

Suddenly Mole tripped and fell, cutting his leg on something sharp. Rat looked to see what it was.

"Hooray! Hooray!" he cried, dancing in the snow. "It's a door-scraper! Don't you see what that means? Well never mind, just help me clear this snow."

The animals set to work, hurling snow in all directions. At last they uncovered a doormat, and then a solid green door. An iron bell-pull hung by its side and below it, on a small brass plate, they could just read the words: MR BADGER.

Mole fell backwards with delight.
Rat hammered on the door. "It's me,
Rat, and my friend, Mole. We've lost
our way in the snow."

Badger opened the door. He was in his
dressing gown. "Come along in," he said
kindly. "There's dinner in the kitchen.
You must stay as long as you like."

Coming Home

$\mathcal{I}$t was a cold December evening. Rat and Mole were on their way home after a long day's outing with Otter. The shadows of night were closing in on them as they passed a crowded sheep-pen and headed for the lights of a nearby village.

Each glowing window held a different scene. At one they saw a birdcage silhouetted against the glass. Its fluffy occupant was fast asleep on his perch. Shivering, Rat and Mole remembered that they still had far to go and they hurried off into the fields again.

Then Mole stopped suddenly. An old, familiar, half-forgotten smell had come to him. It was the smell of home!

"Wait, Ratty, wait!" he cried.

But Rat kept plodding on. Mole ran behind him, torn with grief. At last Rat turned and saw his sobbing friend.

"What's up?" he asked.

"You wouldn't stop!" wailed Mole. "I smelled my home back there. My old home that I left so long ago. It must be somewhere near!"

Rat started back along the path at once. "Come on, old chap!" he said. "We'll find that home of yours!"

Mole soon discovered a familiar
tunnel leading underground. Rat followed
him down until they reached an open
courtyard decorated with statues, hanging
baskets and an ornamental pond. In front
of them was a small front door.

Mole hurried happily through the door and lit a lamp inside. But when he saw the thick dust everywhere and the cheerless, deserted look of his long-neglected house he collapsed with his nose on his paws.

"Oh Ratty!" he cried dismally. "Why did I bring you here?"

But Rat wasn't having any of it. "What a fantastic little house this is!" he called out cheerily. "Now you get a dust rag, Mole, while I light a fire."

In no time at all the house was clean and warm and Rat was busy foraging in the cupboards for dinner.

Just then they heard the murmur of tiny voices in the courtyard. "It must be the field mice," said Mole. "They come here every year."

As Rat opened the door the mice began to sing, filling the air with the joyful sound of a Christmas carol.

"Well sung, boys!" cried Rat heartily. "Come inside!"

"But Ratty," whispered Mole, "we've nothing to give them!"

"Leave that to me," said Rat.

He summoned one of the field mice and, after a short conversation followed by the chink of coins, sent him off with a large shopping basket.

The rest of the field mice perched
in a row on the fireside chair while Rat
prepared some hot mulled ale.

Soon the mice were sipping and coughing and laughing and forgetting they had ever been cold in their lives. Mole tried to persuade one mouse to recite some verse, but he was very shy.

The reluctant performer was saved from his ordeal when the field mouse with the basket reappeared, staggering under the weight of his purchases, and a few minutes later dinner was ready.

Mole sat at the head of the table listening to all the local gossip and thinking what a happy homecoming this had turned out to be after all.

After Rat and Mole had waved
goodbye to their guests, Mole lay
peacefully in his bunk and looked around
the room. He could never abandon his
new life of sun and air and open spaces,
but now he knew his dear old house
would wait and welcome him whenever
he came home.

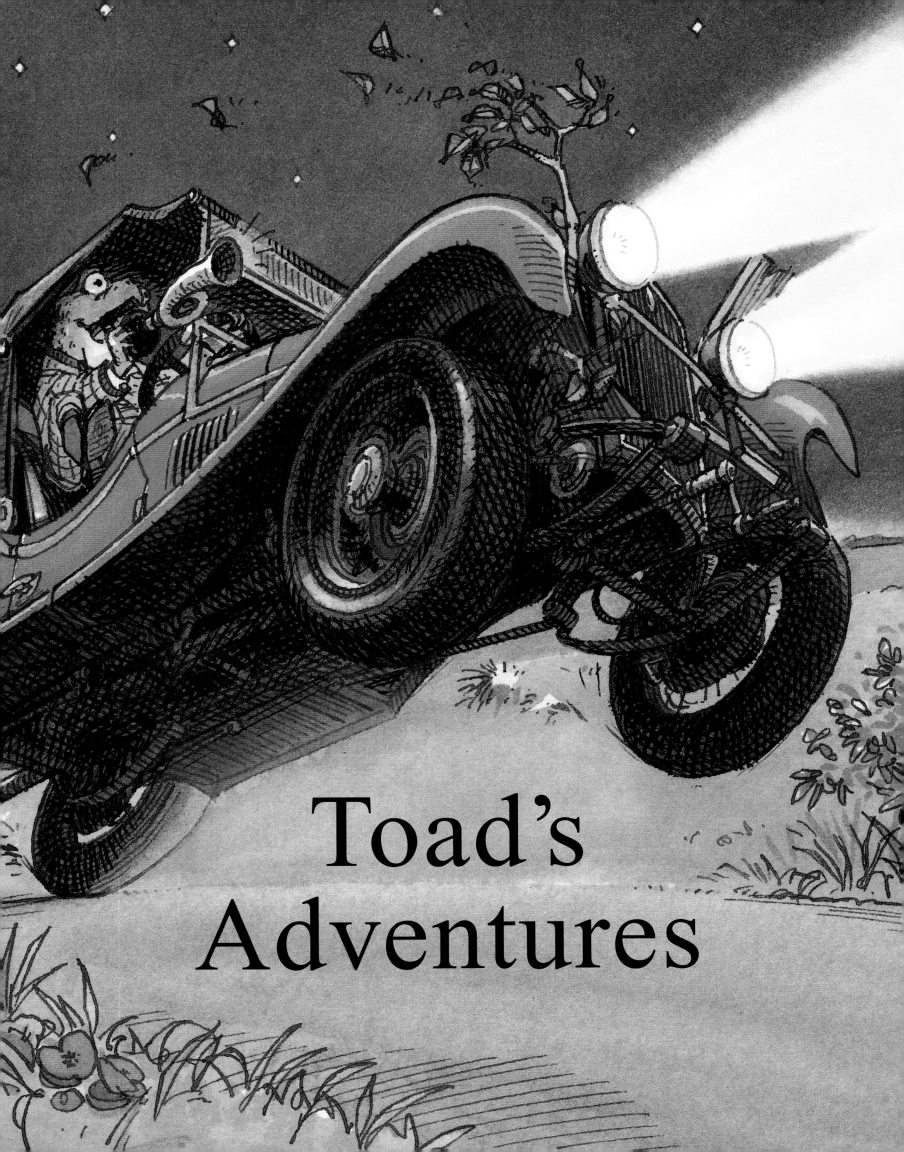

Toad's
Adventures

*E*ver since Toad was bitten by the driving bug he spent his days speeding furiously around the countryside in a succession of shiny new cars. He was a hopelessly bad driver and was always having accidents. He'd been in hospital three times and was constantly in trouble with the police.

One morning, as Rat and Mole were finishing breakfast, a heavy knock sounded at the door. It was Badger.

"The hour has come!" he declared. "Winter is over and it's time to take Toad in hand. We must rescue him from this madness before it's too late."

They met Toad swaggering down the steps of Toad Hall towards a large red motorcar (red was his favorite color).

"Hello you fellows!" he cried. "You're just in time to come for a jolly – er – a jolly…" His words faded as he saw the solemn faces of his friends.

Inside the house Badger spoke sternly, making Toad weep with shame. "You must promise to give up motorcars altogether, Toad," he said.

"Certainly not!" cried Toad, forgetting his tears. "Poop-poop! I never will!"

"Then we must lock you in your room until you see sense," said Badger. "Take him upstairs, you two."

Toad stayed in his room for days.
Then, one morning, Rat found him lying
in bed, looking pale and weak.

"Are you ill, Toad?" Rat asked
anxiously. "Shall I get a doctor?"

"A doctor… and a lawyer too, please Ratty," murmured Toad in a tiny voice. Rat ran off straight away.

The moment he was gone Toad hopped lightly out of bed, laughing heartily. He knotted his sheets together to make a rope and lowered himself out of the window. Then, taking the opposite direction to Rat, he skipped off, whistling a merry tune.

99

Sometime later Toad came to an inn and went inside for lunch. But half-way through the meal he heard a sound which made him tremble. A motorcar was coming down the road! It turned into the yard and stopped outside. Soon Toad could stand no more.

He slipped out to the courtyard and found the car. "There can't be any harm," he said to himself, "in my just *looking* at it."

He walked slowly around it, deep in thought. "I wonder," he said to himself, "if this sort of car starts easily?"

And before he knew it Toad was out on the open road! "I'm Toad the terror, Lord of the lonely trail!" he shouted as the car leapt forwards, gobbling up the miles. He sped on recklessly, living only for the moment, without a thought of what might happen next…

"Pull yourself together, prisoner, and stand up straight," said the Chairman of the Bench of Magistrates. "You have been found guilty of stealing a valuable motorcar, putting the public in danger and being rude to the police. It's twenty years for you this time – and don't do it again!"

They dragged Toad from the
Court House into a grim old castle…
past soldiers, sentries and men-at-arms…
past the torture chamber and the
private scaffold…

...until at last they reached the door to the darkest dungeon in the heart of the innermost jail.

They led Toad down to his cell and locked the door. Then Toad wept bitter tears. "This is the end of everything," he wailed. "The end of the rich and handsome Toad! How can I hope to see the world outside again?"

Toad was to leave his cell rather sooner than he imagined. But that is another story...

Return
to
Toad Hall

Toad had been sent to prison for twenty years, but a kind-hearted jailer's daughter helped him to escape.

After many adventures, he ended up in the river just outside Rat's house.

Rat helped Toad in, gave him clean
clothes and listened to his story over lunch.

"Don't worry, Rat," said Toad.
"I've had enough adventures now.
I'm going back to Toad Hall to lead
a quiet, steady life."

"You mean to say you haven't heard?"
cried Rat, greatly alarmed. "The Stoats
and Weasels took Toad Hall. They live
there now!"

"Oh *do* they!" said Toad, getting up and grabbing a stick. "I'll jolly well see about that!"

He marched off to his old front gate where he met a ferret with a gun.

"Who goes there?" demanded the ferret sharply. Then – BANG! – a bullet whistled past Toad's head.

But Toad would not give up. He took Rat's boat and set off up the river.

He was just passing under a bridge when – CRASH! – a huge stone fell from above and smashed the bottom of the boat. He looked up and saw two stoats laughing heartily.

That night Badger and Mole arrived.

"Well, Toad," said Badger, "there are sentries guarding every gate. We can't get past them – but I have a plan. Your father told me just before he died that there's a secret passage underground. It leads right to the middle of Toad Hall! Tomorrow evening," he went on, "they're going to have a party in the Hall. They'll all be in the dining room unarmed. So I suggest we go down through the tunnel…"

"With our pistols, swords and sticks!" added Rat.

"And whack 'em and whack 'em and whack 'em!" cried Toad.

So the next night, as soon as it grew dark, Rat summoned them to the parlor and proceeded to give out their weapons. Each animal had a sword, a cutlass, a pair of pistols and a policeman's baton! Finally, with Badger leading, they set off along the secret passage.

They groped and shuffled their way along until they heard the sound of shouting, cheering and stamping overhead.

Then they found a trap door and hoisted one another up.

In the next room they heard a weasel shout, "I'll sing you a song about *modest* Toad!" while the others laughed and jeered.

"Follow me!" cried Badger and he flung open the door. The four heroes strode into the room brandishing their weapons.

What a squealing and a screeching filled the air! Tables fell over, china smashed as weasels fled this way and that – through windows, up chimneys – anywhere to escape from those terrible sticks.

In five minutes the room was cleared.
Through broken windows they could hear
the shrieks of terrified stoats and weasels
running off across the lawn.

A few were taken prisoner.

They were told to clean the house
completely and get the bedrooms ready
for the night.

Next day the animals agreed to hold
a banquet of their own in honor of Toad's
return.

"But Toad," warned Rat, "no speeches
and no songs, no boasting of any sort.
You must turn over a new leaf sooner
or later, you know, and now seems a
perfect time to start."

So, just before the banquet, Toad
went to his room and sang a last, loud,
boastful song. Then he came down as
modest as could be.

He didn't talk about himself at all
and would accept no praise. To his
astonished friends it seemed he was
indeed an altered Toad!